For Mommy Bears everywhere ~ A R

For Jenny, the best big sister in the world,
and for our mom ~ A E

Copyright © 2009 by Good Books, Intercourse, PA 17534
International Standard Book Number: 978-1-56148-657-1

Library of Congress Catalog Card Number: 2008029722

Text copyright © Alison Ritchie 2009
Illustrations copyright © Alison Edgson 2009
Original edition published in English by Little Tiger Press,
an imprint of Magi Publications, London, England, 2009.

Printed in China

Library of Congress Cataloging-in-Publication Data
Ritchie, Alison.
Me and my mom! / Alison Ritchie ; illustrated by Alison Edgson.
p. cm.
Summary: Rhyming text describes a day of fun and adventure that a bear shares with his mother.
ISBN 978-1-56148-657-1 (hardcover : alk. paper)
[1. Stories in rhyme. 2. Mother and child--Fiction. 3. Bears--Fiction.] I. Edgson, Alison, ill. II. Title.
PZ8.3.R486Mg 2009
[E]--dc22
2008029722

Me and My Mom!

Alison Ritchie

illustrated by Alison Edgson

Good Books

Intercourse, PA 17534
800/762-7171
www.GoodBooks.com

Me and my mom
are together all day.
I follow her footsteps
as we go out to play.

We make strings of flowers
and Mom is so clever
That *her* daisy chain
seems to go on forever!

We roar in the cave
and it answers our call
With magical echoes —
one big and one small.

GRRR!

GRRR!

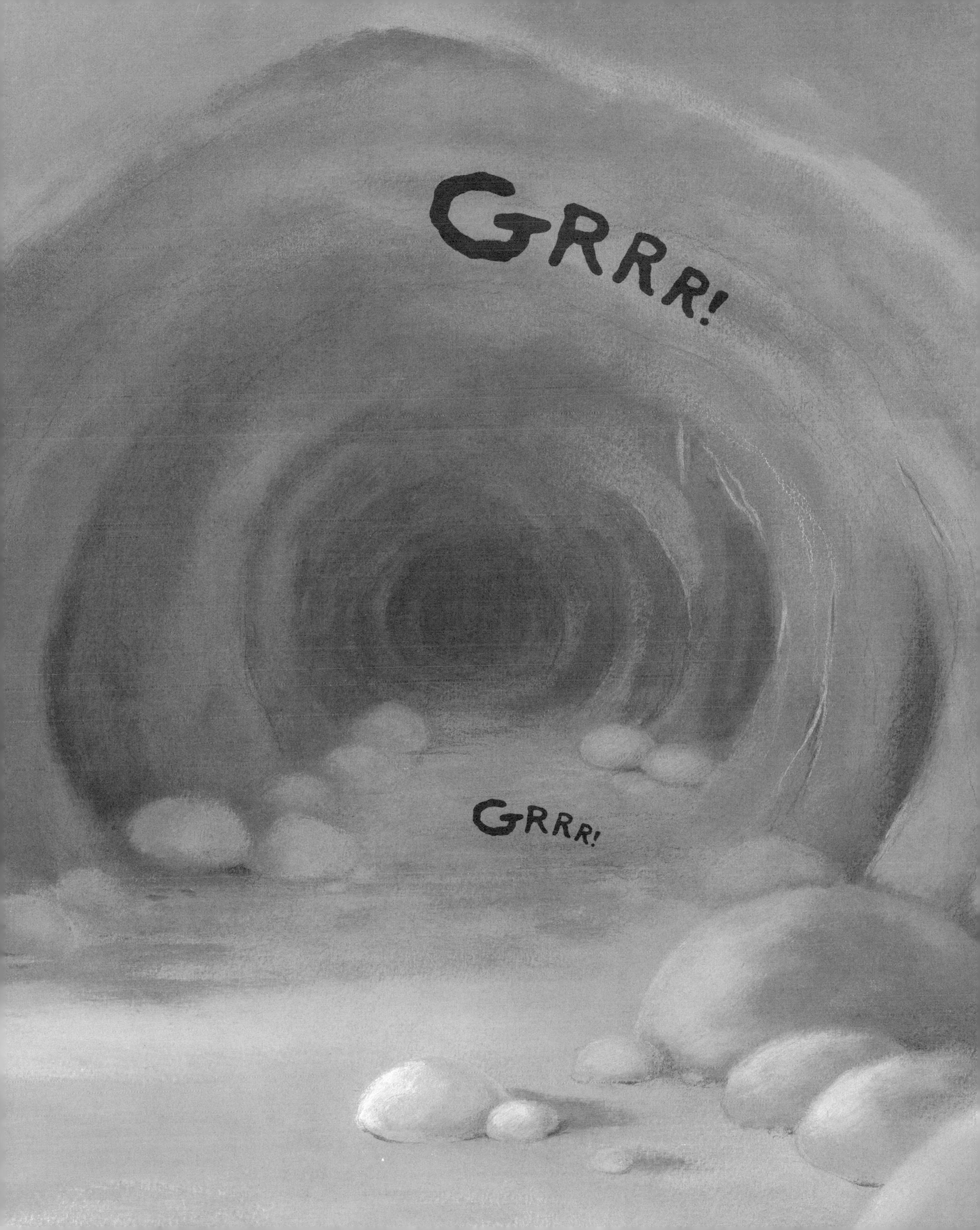
GRRR!
GRRR!

My mom's not afraid
of the dark or the night.
And I'm brave like her
when she's holding me tight!

We know a good trick,
my mommy and me –
I balance one apple
and Mom can do three!

The ice is so slippery,
it's easy to fall.
But soon, just like Mom,
I won't tumble at all!

We glide through the water
and I make a wish
That one day, like Mom,
I will swim like a fish!

With a showery spray
my mom dries her fur.
I wiggle my bottom
and shake just like her.

It's a long way to jump —
I'm not sure if I dare.
But I know I'll be safe
with my mommy right there!

We scoop up some leaves
and throw them up high,
Then watch as they float
gently down from the sky.

From my soft, furry ears
to the tips of my toes,
Mom says I'm the best little
bear cub she knows!

My mom is so special
in every way.
I want to be just like
my mommy one day.